The Philosopher's Joke

By

Jerome K. Jerome

British Library Cataloguing-in-Publication Data
A catalogue record for this book is available from the
British Library

Jerome K. Jerome

Jerome Klapka Jerome was born in Walsall, England in 1859. Both his parents died while he was in his early teens, and he was forced to quit school to support himself. Jerome worked for a number of years collecting coal along railway tracks, before trying his hand at acting, journalism, teaching and soliciting. At long last, in 1885, he had some success with *On the Stage – and Off*, a comic memoir of his experiences with an acting troupe. Jerome produced a number of essays over the following years, and married in 1888, spending the honeymoon in "a little boat" on the Thames.

In 1889, Jerome published his most successful and best-remembered work, *Three Men in a Boat*. Featuring himself and two of his friends encountering humorous situations while floating down the Thames in a small boat, the book was an instant success, and has never been out of print. In fact, its popularity was such that the number of registered Thames boats went up fifty percent in the year following its publication. With the financial security provided by *Three Men in a Boat*, Jerome was able to dedicate himself fully to writing, producing eleven more novels and a number of anthologies of short fiction.

In 1926, Jerome published his autobiography, *My Life and Times*. He died a year later, aged 68.

Myself, I do not believe this story. Six persons are persuaded of its truth; and the hope of these six is to convince themselves it was an hallucination. Their difficulty is there are six of them. Each one alone perceives clearly that it never could have been. Unfortunately, they are close friends, and cannot get away from one another; and when they meet and look into each other's eyes the thing takes shape again.

The one who told it to me, and who immediately wished he had not, was Armitage. He told it to me one night when he and I were the only occupants of the Club smoking-room. His telling me—as he explained afterwards—was an impulse of the moment. Sense of the thing had been pressing upon him all that day with unusual persistence; and the idea had occurred to him, on my entering the room, that the flippant scepticism with which an essentially commonplace mind like my own—he used the words in no offensive sense—would be sure to regard the affair might help to direct his own attention to its more absurd aspect. I am inclined to think it did. He thanked me for dismissing his entire narrative as the delusion of a disordered brain, and begged me not to mention the matter to another living soul. I promised; and I may as well here observe that I do not call this mentioning the matter. Armitage is not the man's real name; it does not even begin with an A. You might read this story and dine next to him the same evening: you would know nothing.

Also, of course, I did not consider myself debarred from speaking about it, discreetly, to Mrs. Armitage, a charming woman. She burst into tears at the first mention of the thing. It took me all I knew to tranquillize her. She said that when she did not think about the thing she could be happy. She and Armitage never spoke of it to one another; and left to themselves her opinion was that eventually they might put remembrance behind them. She wished they were not quite so friendly with the Everetts. Mr. and Mrs. Everett had both dreamt precisely the same dream; that is, assuming it was a dream. Mr. Everett was not the sort of person that a clergyman ought, perhaps, to know; but as Armitage would always argue: for a teacher of Christianity to withdraw his friendship from a man because that man was somewhat of a sinner would be inconsistent. Rather should he remain his friend and seek to influence him. They dined with the Everetts regularly on Tuesdays, and sitting opposite the Everetts, it seemed impossible to accept as a fact that all four of them at the same time and in the same manner had fallen victims to the same illusion. I think I succeeded in leaving her more hopeful. She acknowledged that the story, looked at from the point of common sense, did sound ridiculous; and threatened me that if I ever breathed a word of it to anyone, she never would speak to me again. She is a charming woman, as I have already mentioned.

By a curious coincidence I happened at the time to be one of Everett's directors on a Company he had just promoted for taking over and developing the Red Sea

Coasting trade. I lunched with him the following Sunday. He is an interesting talker, and curiosity to discover how so shrewd a man would account for his connection with so insane—so impossible a fancy, prompted me to hint my knowledge of the story. The manner both of him and of his wife changed suddenly. They wanted to know who it was had told me. I refused the information, because it was evident they would have been angry with him. Everett's theory was that one of them had dreamt it—probably Camelford—and by hypnotic suggestion had conveyed to the rest of them the impression that they had dreamt it also. He added that but for one slight incident he should have ridiculed from the very beginning the argument that it could have been anything else than a dream. But what that incident was he would not tell me. His object, as he explained, was not to dwell upon the business, but to try and forget it. Speaking as a friend, he advised me, likewise, not to cackle about the matter any more than I could help, lest trouble should arise with regard to my director's fees. His way of putting things is occasionally blunt.

It was at the Everetts', later on, that I met Mrs. Camelford, one of the handsomest women I have ever set eyes upon. It was foolish of me, but my memory for names is weak. I forgot that Mr. and Mrs. Camelford were the other two concerned, and mentioned the story as a curious tale I had read years ago in an old Miscellany. I had reckoned on it to lead me into a discussion with her on platonic friendship. She jumped up from her chair and gave me a look. I remembered then, and could have bitten out my tongue. It took me a long while to make my peace, but she came round in the end, consenting to attribute my blunder to mere stupidity. She was quite convinced herself, she told me, that the thing was pure imagination. It was only when in company with the others that any doubt as to this crossed her mind. Her own idea was that, if everybody would agree never to mention the matter again, it would end in their forgetting it. She supposed it was her husband who had been my informant: he was just that sort of ass. She did not say it unkindly. She said when she was first married, ten years ago, few people had a more irritating effect upon her than had Camelford; but that since she had seen more of other men she had come to respect him. I like to hear a woman speak well of her husband. It is a departure which, in my opinion, should be more encouraged than it is. I assured her Camelford was not the culprit; and on the understanding that I might come to see her—not too often—on her Thursdays, I agreed with her that the best thing I could do would be to dismiss the subject from my mind and occupy myself instead with questions that concerned myself.

I had never talked much with Camelford before that time, though I had often seen him at the Club. He is a strange man, of whom many stories are told. He writes journalism for a living, and poetry, which he publishes at his own expense, apparently for recreation. It occurred to me that his theory would at all events be interesting; but at first he would not talk at all, pretending to ignore the whole affair, as idle nonsense. I had almost despaired of drawing him out, when one evening, of his own accord, he asked me if I thought Mrs. Armitage, with whom he knew I was on terms of friendship, still attached importance to the thing. On my expressing the opinion that Mrs. Armitage was the most troubled of the group, he was irritated; and urged me to leave the rest of them alone and devote whatever sense I might possess to persuading her in particular that the entire thing was and could be nothing but pure myth. He confessed frankly that to him it was still a mystery. He could easily regard it as chimera, but for one slight incident. He would not for a long while say what that was, but there is such a thing as perseverance, and in the end I dragged it out of him. This is what he told me.

"We happened by chance to find ourselves alone in the conservatory, that night of the ball—we six. Most of the crowd had already left. The last 'extra' was being played: the music came to us faintly. Stooping to pick up Jessica's fan, which she had let fall to the ground, something shining on the tesselated pavement underneath a group of palms suddenly caught my eye. We had not said a word to one another; indeed, it was the first evening we had any of us met one another—that is, unless the thing was not a dream. I picked it up. The others gathered round me, and when we looked into one another's eyes we understood: it was a broken wine-cup, a curious goblet of Bavarian glass. It was the goblet out of which we had all dreamt that we had drunk."

I have put the story together as it seems to me it must have happened. The incidents, at all events, are facts. Things have since occurred to those concerned affording me hope that they will never read it. I should not have troubled to tell it at all, but that it has a moral.

Six persons sat round the great oak table in the wainscoted *Speise Saal* of that cosy hostelry, the Kneiper Hof at Konigsberg. It was late into the night. Under ordinary circumstances they would have been in bed, but having arrived by the last train from Dantzic, and having supped on German fare, it had seemed to them discreeter to remain awhile in talk. The house was strangely silent. The rotund landlord, leaving their candles ranged upon the sideboard, had wished them "Gute Nacht" an hour before. The spirit of the ancient house enfolded them within its wings.

Here in this very chamber, if rumour is to be believed, Emmanuel Kant himself had sat discoursing many a time and oft. The walls, behind which for more than forty years the little peak-faced man had thought and worked, rose silvered by the moonlight just across the narrow way; the three high windows of the *Speise Saal* give out upon the old Cathedral tower beneath which now he rests. Philosophy, curious concerning human phenomena, eager for experience, unhampered by the limitation Convention would impose upon all speculation, was in the smoky air.

"Not into future events," remarked the Rev. Nathaniel Armitage, "it is better they should be hidden from us. But into the future of ourselves—our temperament, our character—I think we ought to be allowed to see. At twenty we are one individual; at forty, another person entirely, with other views, with other interests, a different outlook upon life, attracted by quite other attributes, repelled by the very qualities that once attracted us. It is extremely awkward, for all of us."

"I am glad to hear somebody else say that," observed Mrs. Everett, in her gentle, sympathetic voice. "I have thought it all myself so often. Sometimes I have blamed myself, yet how can one help it: the things that appeared of importance to us, they become indifferent; new voices call to us; the idols we once worshipped, we see their feet of clay."

"If under the head of idols you include me," laughed the jovial Mr. Everett, "don't hesitate to say so." He was a large red-faced gentleman, with small twinkling eyes, and a mouth both strong and sensuous. "I didn't make my feet myself. I never asked anybody to take me for a stained-glass saint. It is not I who have changed."

"I know, dear, it is I," his thin wife answered with a meek smile. "I was beautiful, there was no doubt about it, when you married me."

"You were, my dear," agreed her husband: "As a girl few could hold a candle to you."

"It was the only thing about me that you valued, my beauty," continued his wife; "and it went so quickly. I feel sometimes as if I had swindled you."

"But there is a beauty of the mind, of the soul," remarked the Rev. Nathaniel Armitage, "that to some men is more attractive than mere physical perfection."

The soft eyes of the faded lady shone for a moment with the light of pleasure. "I am afraid Dick is not of that number," she sighed.

"Well, as I said just now about my feet," answered her husband genially, "I didn't make myself. I always have been a slave to beauty and always shall be. There would be no sense in pretending among chums that you haven't lost your looks, old girl." He laid his fine hand with kindly intent upon her bony shoulder. "But there is no call for you to fret yourself as if you had done it on purpose. No one but a lover imagines a woman growing more beautiful as she grows older."

"Some women would seem to," answered his wife.

Involuntarily she glanced to where Mrs. Camelford sat with elbows resting on the table; and involuntarily also the small twinkling eyes of her husband followed in the same direction. There is a type that reaches its prime in middle age. Mrs. Camelford, *nee* Jessica Dearwood, at twenty had been an uncanny-looking creature, the only thing about her appealing to general masculine taste having been her magnificent eyes, and even these had frightened more than they had allured. At forty, Mrs. Camelford might have posed for the entire Juno.

"Yes, he's a cunning old joker is Time," murmured Mr. Everett, almost inaudibly.

"What ought to have happened," said Mrs. Armitage, while with deft fingers rolling herself a cigarette, "was for you and Nellie to have married."

Mrs. Everett's pale face flushed scarlet.

"My dear," exclaimed the shocked Nathaniel Armitage, flushing likewise.

"Oh, why may one not sometimes speak the truth?" answered his wife petulantly. "You and I are utterly unsuited to one another—everybody sees it. At nineteen it seemed to me beautiful, holy, the idea of being a clergyman's wife, fighting by his side against evil. Besides, you have changed since then. You were human, my dear Nat, in those days, and the best dancer I had ever met. It was your dancing was your chief attraction for me as likely as not, if I had only known myself. At nineteen how can one know oneself?"

"We loved each other," the Rev. Armitage reminded her.

"I know we did, passionately—then; but we don't now." She laughed a little bitterly. "Poor Nat! I am only another trial added to your long list. Your beliefs, your ideals are meaningless to me—mere narrow-minded dogmas, stifling thought. Nellie was the wife Nature had intended for you, so soon as she had lost her beauty and with it all her worldly ideas. Fate was maturing her for you, if only we had known. As for me, I ought to have been the wife of an artist, of a poet." Unconsciously a glance from her ever restless eyes flashed across the table to where Horatio Camelford sat, puffing clouds of smoke into the air from a huge black meerschaum pipe. "Bohemia is my country. Its poverty, its struggle would have been a joy to me. Breathing its free air, life would have been worth living."

Horatio Camelford leant back with eyes fixed on the oaken ceiling. "It is a mistake," said Horatio Camelford, "for the artist ever to marry."

The handsome Mrs. Camelford laughed good-naturedly. "The artist," remarked Mrs. Camelford, "from what I have seen of him would never know the inside of his shirt from the outside if his wife was not there to take it out of the drawer and put it over his head."

"His wearing it inside out would not make much difference to the world," argued her husband. "The sacrifice of his art to the necessity of keeping his wife and family does."

"Well, you at all events do not appear to have sacrificed much, my boy," came the breezy voice of Dick Everett. "Why, all the world is ringing with your name."

"When I am forty-one, with all the best years of my life behind me," answered the Poet. "Speaking as a man, I have nothing to regret. No one could have had a better wife; my children are charming. I have lived the peaceful existence of the successful citizen. Had I been true to my trust I should have gone out into the wilderness, the only possible home of the teacher, the prophet. The artist is the bridegroom of Art. Marriage for him is an immorality. Had I my time again I should remain a bachelor."

"Time brings its revenges, you see," laughed Mrs. Camelford. "At twenty that fellow threatened to commit suicide if I would not marry him, and cordially disliking him I consented. Now twenty years later, when I am just getting used to him, he calmly turns round and says he would have been better without me."

"I heard something about it at the time," said Mrs. Armitage. "You were very much in love with somebody else, were you not?"

"Is not the conversation assuming a rather dangerous direction?" laughed Mrs. Camelford.

"I was thinking the same thing," agreed Mrs. Everett. "One would imagine some strange influence had seized upon us, forcing us to speak our thoughts aloud."

"I am afraid I was the original culprit," admitted the Reverend Nathaniel. "This room is becoming quite oppressive. Had we not better go to bed?"

The ancient lamp suspended from its smoke-grimed beam uttered a faint, gurgling sob, and spluttered out. The shadow of the old Cathedral tower crept in and stretched across the room, now illuminated only by occasional beams from the cloud-curtained moon. At the other end of the table sat a peak-faced little gentleman, clean-shaven, in full-bottomed wig.

"Forgive me," said the little gentleman. He spoke in English, with a strong accent. "But it seems to me here is a case where two parties might be of service to one another."

The six fellow-travellers round the table looked at one another, but none spoke. The idea that came to each of them, as they explained to one another later, was that without remembering it they had taken their candles and had gone to bed. This was surely a dream.

"It would greatly assist me," continued the little peak-faced gentleman, "in experiments I am conducting into the phenomena of human tendencies, if you would allow me to put your lives back twenty years."

Still no one of the six replied. It seemed to them that the little old gentleman must have been sitting there among them all the time, unnoticed by them.

"Judging from your talk this evening," continued the peak-faced little gentleman, "you should welcome my offer. You appear to me to be one and all of exceptional intelligence. You perceive the mistakes that you have made: you understand the causes. The future veiled, you could not help yourselves. What I propose to do is to put you back twenty years. You will be boys and girls again, but with this difference: that the knowledge of the future, so far as it relates to yourselves, will remain with you.

"Come," urged the old gentleman, "the thing is quite simple of accomplishment. As—as a certain philosopher has clearly proved: the universe is only the result of our own perceptions. By what may appear to you to be magic—by what in reality will be simply a chemical operation—I remove from your memory the events of the last twenty years, with the exception of what immediately concerns your own personalities. You will retain all knowledge of the changes, physical and mental, that will be in store for you; all else will pass from your perception."

The little old gentleman took a small phial from his waistcoat pocket, and, filling one of the massive wine-glasses from a decanter, measured into it some half-a-dozen drops. Then he placed the glass in the centre of the table.

"Youth is a good time to go back to," said the peak-faced little gentleman, with a smile. "Twenty years ago, it was the night of the Hunt Ball. You remember it?"

It was Everett who drank first. He drank it with his little twinkling eyes fixed hungrily on the proud handsome face of Mrs. Camelford; and then handed the glass to his wife. It was she perhaps who drank from it most eagerly. Her life with Everett, from the day when she had risen from a bed of sickness stripped of all her beauty, had been one bitter wrong. She drank with the wild hope that the thing might possibly be not a dream; and thrilled to the touch of the man she loved, as reaching across the table he took the glass from her hand. Mrs. Armitage was the fourth to drink. She took the cup from her husband, drank with a quiet smile, and passed it on to Camelford. And Camelford drank, looking at nobody, and replaced the glass upon the table.

"Come," said the little old gentleman to Mrs. Camelford, "you are the only one left. The whole thing will be incomplete without you."

"I have no wish to drink," said Mrs. Camelford, and her eyes sought those of her husband, but he would not look at her.

"Come," again urged the Figure. And then Camelford looked at her and laughed drily.

"You had better drink," he said. "It's only a dream."

"If you wish it," she answered. And it was from his hands she took the glass.

It is from the narrative as Armitage told it to me that night in the Club smoking-room that I am taking most of my material. It seemed to him that all things began slowly to rise upward, leaving him stationary, but with a great pain as though the inside of him were being torn away—the same sensation greatly exaggerated, so he likened it, as descending in a lift. But around him all the time was silence and darkness unrelieved. After a period that might have been minutes, that might have been years, a faint light crept towards him. It grew stronger, and into the air which now fanned his cheek there stole the sound of far-off music. The light and the music both increased, and one by one his senses came back to him. He was seated on a low cushioned bench beneath a group of palms. A young girl was sitting beside him, but her face was turned away from him.

"I did not catch your name," he was saying. "Would you mind telling it to me?"

She turned her face towards him. It was the most spiritually beautiful face he had ever seen. "I am in the same predicament," she laughed. "You had better write yours on my programme, and I will write mine on yours."

So they wrote upon each other's programme and exchanged again. The name she had written was Alice Blatchley.

He had never seen her before, that he could remember. Yet at the back of his mind there dwelt the haunting knowledge of her. Somewhere long ago they had met, talked together. Slowly, as one recalls a dream, it came back to him. In some other life, vague, shadowy, he had married this woman. For the first few years they had loved each other; then the gulf had opened between them, widened. Stern, strong voices had called to him to lay aside his selfish dreams, his boyish ambitions, to take upon his shoulders the yoke of a great duty. When more than ever he had demanded sympathy and help, this woman had fallen away from him. His ideals but irritated her. Only at the cost of daily bitterness had he been able to resist her endeavours to draw him from his path. A face—that of a woman with soft eyes, full of helpfulness, shone through the mist of his dream—the face of a woman who would one day come to him out of the Future with outstretched hands that he would yearn to clasp.

"Shall we not dance?" said the voice beside him. "I really won't sit out a waltz."

They hurried into the ball-room. With his arm about her form, her wondrous eyes shyly, at rare moments, seeking his, then vanishing again behind their drooping lashes, the brain, the mind, the very soul of the young man passed out of his own keeping. She complimented him in her bewitching manner, a delightful blending of condescension and timidity.

"You dance extremely well," she told him. "You may ask me for another, later on."

The words flashed out from that dim haunting future. "Your dancing was your chief attraction for me, as likely as not, had I but known?"

All that evening and for many months to come the Present and the Future fought within him. And the experience of Nathaniel Armitage, divinity student, was the experience likewise of Alice Blatchley, who had fallen in love with him at first sight, having found him the divinest dancer she had ever whirled with to the sensuous music of the waltz; of Horatio Camelford, journalist and minor poet, whose journalism earned him a bare income, but at whose minor poetry critics smiled; of Jessica Dearwood, with her glorious eyes, and muddy complexion, and her wild hopeless passion for the big, handsome, ruddy-bearded Dick Everett, who, knowing it, only laughed at her in his kindly, lordly way, telling her with frank brutalness that the woman who was not beautiful had missed her vocation in life; of that scheming, conquering young gentleman himself, who at twenty-five had already made his mark in the City, shrewd, clever, cool-headed as a fox, except where a pretty face and shapely hand or ankle were concerned; of Nellie Fanshawe, then in the pride of her ravishing beauty, who loved none but herself, whose clay-made gods were jewels, and fine dresses and rich feasts, the envy of other women and the courtship of all mankind.

That evening of the ball each clung to the hope that this memory of the future was but a dream. They had been introduced to one another; had heard each other's names for the first time with a start of recognition; had avoided one another's eyes; had hastened to plunge into meaningless talk; till that moment when young Camelford, stooping to pick up Jessica's fan, had found that broken fragment of the Rhenish wine-glass. Then it was that conviction refused to be shaken off, that knowledge of the future had to be sadly accepted.

What they had not foreseen was that knowledge of the future in no way affected their emotions of the present. Nathaniel Armitage grew day by day more hopelessly in love with bewitching Alice Blatchley. The thought of her marrying anyone else—the long-haired, priggish Camelford in particular—sent the blood boiling through his veins; added to which sweet Alice, with her arms about his neck, would confess to him that life without him would be a misery hardly to be endured, that the thought of him as the husband of another woman—of Nellie Fanshawe in particular—was madness to her. It was right perhaps, knowing what they did, that they should say good-bye to one another. She would bring sorrow into his life. Better far that he should put her away from him, that she should die of a broken heart, as she felt sure she would. How could he, a fond lover, inflict this suffering upon her? He ought of course to marry Nellie Fanshawe, but he could not bear the girl. Would it not be the height of absurdity to marry a girl he strongly disliked because twenty years hence she might be more suitable to him than the woman he now loved and who loved him?

Nor could Nellie Fanshawe bring herself to discuss without laughter the suggestion of marrying on a hundred-and-fifty a year a curate that she positively hated. There would come a time when wealth would be indifferent to her, when her exalted spirit would ask but for the satisfaction of self-sacrifice. But that time had not arrived. The emotions it would bring with it she could not in her present state even imagine. Her whole present being craved for the things of this world, the things that were within her grasp. To ask her to forego them now because later on she would not care for them! it was like telling a schoolboy to avoid the tuck-shop because, when a man, the thought of stick-jaw would be nauseous to him. If her capacity for enjoyment was to be short-lived, all the more reason for grasping joy quickly.

Alice Blatchley, when her lover was not by, gave herself many a headache trying to think the thing out logically. Was it not foolish of her to rush into this marriage with dear Nat? At forty she would wish she had married somebody else. But most women at forty—she judged from conversation round about her—wished they had married somebody else. If every girl at twenty listened to herself at forty there would be no more marriage. At forty she would be a different person altogether. That other elderly person did not interest her. To ask a young girl to spoil her life purely in the interests of this middle-aged party—it did not seem right. Besides, whom else was she to marry? Camelford would not have her; he did not want her then; he was not going to want her at forty. For practical purposes Camelford was out of the question. She might marry somebody else altogether—and fare worse. She might remain a spinster: she hated the mere name of spinster. The inky-fingered woman journalist that, if all went well, she might become: it was not her idea. Was she acting selfishly? Ought she, in his own interests, to refuse to marry dear Nat? Nellie—the little cat—who would suit him at forty, would not have him. If he was going to marry anyone but Nellie he might as well marry her, Alice. A bachelor clergyman! it sounded almost improper. Nor was dear Nat the type. If she threw him over it would be into the arms of some designing minx. What was she to do?

Camelford at forty, under the influence of favourable criticism, would have persuaded himself he was a heaven-sent prophet, his whole life to be beautifully spent in the saving of mankind. At twenty he felt he wanted to live. Weird-looking Jessica, with her magnificent eyes veiling mysteries, was of more importance to him than the rest of the species combined. Knowledge of the future in his ease only spurred desire. The muddy complexion would grow pink and white, the thin limbs round and shapely; the now scornful eyes would one day light with love at his coming. It was what he had once hoped: it was what he now knew. At forty the artist is stronger than the man; at twenty the man is stronger than the artist.

An uncanny creature, so most folks would have described Jessica Dearwood. Few would have imagined her developing into the good-natured, easy-going Mrs. Camelford of middle age. The animal, so strong within her at twenty, at thirty had burnt itself out. At eighteen, madly, blindly in love with red-bearded, deep-voiced Dick Everett she would, had he whistled to her, have flung herself gratefully at his feet, and this in spite of the knowledge forewarning her of the miserable life he would certainly lead her, at all events until her slowly developing beauty should give her the whip hand of him—by which time she would have come to despise him. Fortunately, as she told herself, there was no fear of his doing so, the future notwithstanding. Nellie Fanshawe's beauty held him as with chains of steel, and Nellie had no intention of allowing her rich prize to escape her. Her own lover, it was true, irritated her more than any man she had ever met, but at least he would afford her refuge from the bread of charity. Jessica Dearwood, an orphan, had been brought up by a distant relative. She had not been the child to win affection. Of silent, brooding nature, every thoughtless incivility had been to her an insult, a wrong. Acceptance of young Camelford seemed her only escape from a life that had become to her a martyrdom. At forty-one he would wish he had remained a bachelor; but at thirty-eight that would not trouble her. She would know herself he was much better off as he was. Meanwhile, she would have come to like him, to respect him. He would be famous, she would be proud of him. Crying into her pillow—she could not help it—for love of handsome Dick, it was still a comfort to reflect that Nellie Fanshawe, as it were, was watching over her, protecting her from herself.

Dick, as he muttered to himself a dozen times a day, ought to marry Jessica. At thirty-eight she would be his ideal. He looked at her as she was at eighteen, and shuddered. Nellie at thirty would be plain and uninteresting. But when did consideration of the future ever cry halt to passion: when did a lover ever pause thinking of the morrow? If her beauty was to quickly pass, was not that one reason the more urging him to possess it while it lasted?

Nellie Fanshawe at forty would be a saint. The prospect did not please her: she hated saints. She would love the tiresome, solemn Nathaniel: of what use was that to her now? He did not desire her; he was in love with Alice, and Alice was in love with him. What would be the sense—even if they all agreed—in the three of them making themselves miserable for all their youth that they might be contented in their old age? Let age fend for itself and leave youth to its own instincts. Let elderly saints suffer—it was their *metier*—and youth drink the cup of life. It was a pity Dick was the only "catch" available, but he was young and handsome. Other girls had to put up with sixty and the gout.

Another point, a very serious point, had been overlooked. All that had arrived to them in that dim future of the past had happened to them as the results of their making the marriages they had made. To what fate other roads would lead their knowledge could not tell them. Nellie Fanshawe had become at forty a lovely character. Might not the hard life she had led with her husband—a life calling for continual sacrifice, for daily self-control—have helped towards this end? As the wife of a poor curate of high moral principles, would the same result have been secured? The fever that had robbed her of her beauty and turned her thoughts inward had been the result of sitting out on the balcony of the Paris Opera House with an Italian Count on the occasion of a fancy dress ball. As the wife of an East End clergyman the chances are she would have escaped that fever and its purifying effects. Was there not danger in the position: a supremely beautiful young woman, worldly-minded, hungry for pleasure, condemned to a life of poverty with a man she did not care for? The influence of Alice upon Nathaniel Armitage, during those first years when his character was forming, had been all for good. Could he be sure that, married to Nellie, he might not have deteriorated?

Were Alice Blatchley to marry an artist could she be sure that at forty she would still be in sympathy with artistic ideals? Even as a child had not her desire ever been in the opposite direction to that favoured by her nurse? Did not the reading of Conservative journals invariably incline her towards Radicalism, and the steady stream of Radical talk round her husband's table invariably set her seeking arguments in favour of the feudal system? Might it not have been her husband's growing Puritanism that had driven her to crave for Bohemianism? Suppose that towards middle age, the wife of a wild artist, she suddenly "took religion," as the saying is. Her last state would be worse than the first.

Camelford was of delicate physique. As an absent-minded bachelor with no one to give him his meals, no one to see that his things were aired, could he have lived till forty? Could he be sure that home life had not given more to his art than it had taken from it?

Jessica Dearwood, of a nervous, passionate nature, married to a bad husband, might at forty have posed for one of the Furies. Not until her life had become restful had her good looks shown themselves. Hers was the type of beauty that for its development demands tranquillity.

Dick Everett had no delusions concerning himself. That, had he married Jessica, he could for ten years have remained the faithful husband of a singularly plain wife he knew to be impossible. But Jessica would have been no patient Griselda. The extreme probability was that having married her at twenty for the sake of her beauty at thirty, at twenty-nine at latest she would have divorced him.

Everett was a man of practical ideas. It was he who took the matter in hand. The refreshment contractor admitted that curious goblets of German glass occasionally crept into their stock. One of the waiters, on the understanding that in no case should he be called upon to pay for them, admitted having broken more than one wine-glass on that particular evening: thought it not unlikely he might have attempted to hide the fragments under a convenient palm. The whole thing evidently was a dream. So youth decided at the time, and the three marriages took place within three months of one another.

It was some ten years later that Armitage told me the story that night in the Club smoking-room. Mrs. Everett had just recovered from a severe attack of rheumatic fever, contracted the spring before in Paris. Mrs. Camelford, whom previously I had not met, certainly seemed to me one of the handsomest women I have ever seen. Mrs. Armitage—I knew her when she was Alice Blatchley—I found more charming as a woman than she had been as a girl. What she could have seen in Armitage I never could understand. Camelford made his mark some ten years later: poor fellow, he did not live long to enjoy his fame. Dick Everett has still another six years to work off; but he is well behaved, and there is talk of a petition.

It is a curious story altogether, I admit. As I said at the beginning, I do not myself believe it.